Shifty McGifty
AND SLIPPERY SAM

SWAG

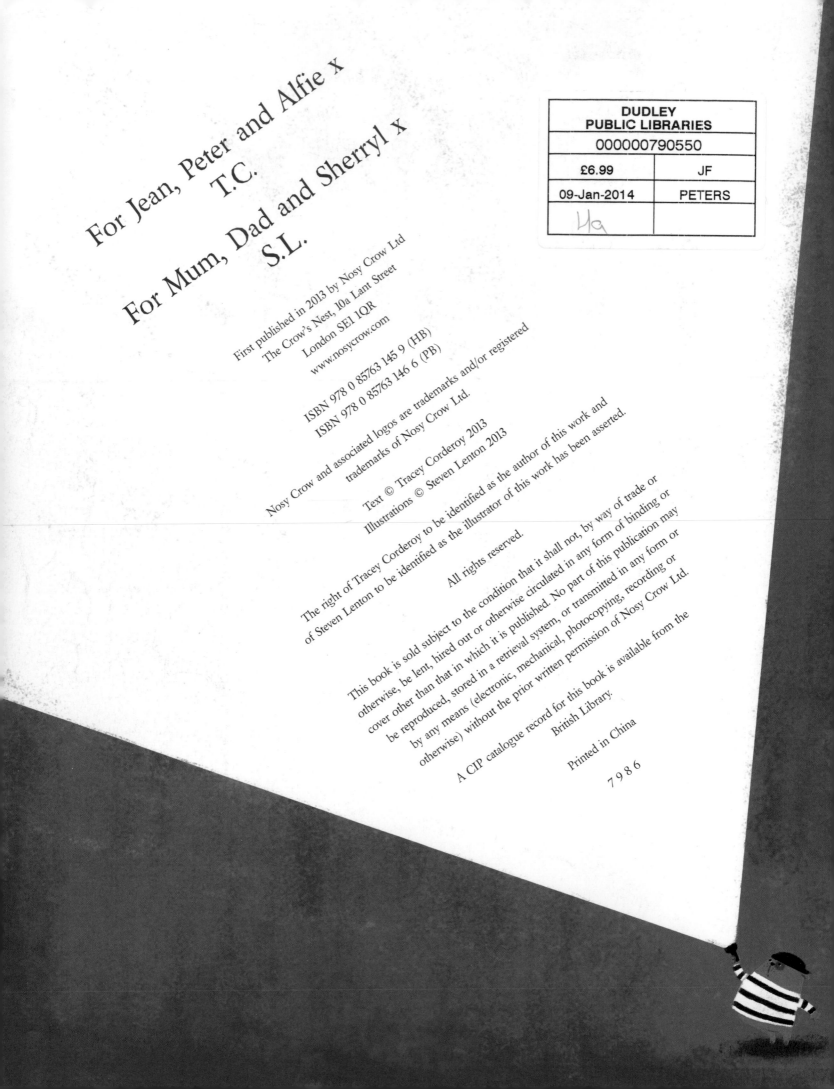

For Jean, Peter and Alfie x
T.C.

For Mum, Dad and Sherryl x
S.L.

First published in 2013 by Nosy Crow Ltd
The Crow's Nest, 10a Lant Street
London SE1 1QR
www.nosycrow.com

ISBN 978 0 85763 145 9 (HB)
ISBN 978 0 85763 146 6 (PB)

Nosy Crow and associated logos are trademarks and/or registered trademarks of Nosy Crow Ltd.

Text © Tracey Corderoy 2013
Illustrations © Steven Lenton 2013

The right of Tracey Corderoy to be identified as the author of this work and of Steven Lenton to be identified as the illustrator of this work has been asserted.

A CIP catalogue record for this book is available from the British Library.

Printed in China

7 9 8 6

Shifty McGifty
AND
Slippery Sam

Tracey Corderoy

Illustrated by

Steven Lenton

In the dead of night,

when the moon yawned down,
two gloomy robber dogs
plodded through town.

They got to their house and they flopped down inside.
"We're no good at robbing at all," Shifty sighed.
He tipped out their swag bag,
but nothing was there . . .

except for a spider
who gave them a scare!

SWAG

"You're right," nodded Sam. "We are bad at this job!
And think of the places we just couldn't rob . . .
the bank and the butcher's, the paper shop too.
The bookshop, the bike shop . . .

. . . and even the ZOO!"

"Hey, we should rob somewhere less tricky," Sam cried.

"Like where?" muttered Shifty. "Where haven't we tried . . .?"

"Our neighbours!" yelled Sam, with a whoop and a shout.

"But hang on," groaned Shifty, "they never go out!"

neighbour dogs

He paced up and down. "We'll invite them to tea!
A **party**," he sniggered. "Oh, clever old me!
And **then**, when the neighbours are here having fun,
we'll sneak to their houses and rob every one!"

us

sneaking

"But parties have food," grumbled Sam. "We can't cook."
"Don't worry!" said Shifty. "We've got this cookbook!"

They started with doughnuts and to their surprise,
they turned out just right, so they cooked some fruit pies.
"Now cupcakes!" cried Shifty. "And let's ice them too!
I never knew baking was fun, Sam. Did you?"

The party day came and the neighbours piled in.
"How lovely!" said one, with a big curly grin.

They gasped with delight when the food was set down.

"So creamy!"

"So dreamy!"

"The best buns in town!"

"Why, thank you," blushed Shifty.

"It's nothing!" beamed Sam.

"Would you care for a doughnut

with raspberry jam?"

"Now's our moment," hissed Shifty.
"They're all drinking tea.
We need to get **robbing**,
I think – follow me!"

As they sneaked through
the window, they hadn't a clue
that a neighbour had heard
what they wanted to do.

"They're **thieves**!" he said crossly.
"I think that it's time
that we all put a stop
to this terrible crime."

As the robber dogs went to see what they could find,

all of their neighbours were creeping behind.

"Oh, WOW!" whispered Sam, as they slunk through a door.

They'd never seen so many goodies before!

Then all of a sudden,
the door opened wide.
"No you don't!"
yelled their neighbours,
bursting inside.

But the Scottie dog suddenly started to sob.
"My teddy!" he sniffled. "They stole Big-Eared Bob!"
"Don't cry," pleaded Shifty,
and Sam turned quite pink.
"We're sorry," they murmured.
"We just . . . didn't think."

"We see now that robbing makes everyone sad.
But we still need a job . . . just a job that's not bad."
"I know!" cried the sausage dog, nodding his head.
"Why don't you open a café instead?"

"A café?" gasped Shifty.
"Do you think that we could?"

"Oh, yes!" cried the others.
"You'd be **really good!**"

So the very next week on the town's busy street,
their new café opened – all shiny and neat.
It had white polished tables
and chairs with pink hearts.
And it served yummy cupcakes
and little jam tarts!

SALES
£2.00

"Oh, wow, Sam," grinned Shifty. "Just look at that queue!
All our neighbours are waiting . . . and other dogs too!"
Sam peered from the window and fluffed up his hat.
"No more robbing!" he nodded.
"We're done with all that!"

Now Shifty and Sam never grumble or groan.
They **love** baking cakes and they leave crime alone.
And as for their swag bag,
I'm happy to say . . .

. . . they crumpled it up and they chucked it away!